P9-DEU-768
#1
BEST IN SHOW

BY TOM ANGLEBERGER

ILLUSTRATED BY CECE BELL

THE GOAT WHO CHEWED TOO MUCH

Cataloging-in-Publication Data has been applied for and may be obtained from the Library of Congress.

Hardcover ISBN: 978-1-4197-0956-2
Paperback ISBN: 978-1-4197-0967-8

Book design by Pamela Notarantonio

With special thanks to Kwame Alexander.

Printed and bound in U.S.A.
10 9 8 7 6 5 4 3 2

ABRAMS The Art of Books
115 West 18th Street, New York, NY 10011
abramsbooks.com

For Tony, Ang, and
Sophia DiTerlizzi, with love

CONTENTS

PART 1
Inspector Flytrap in
The Taking of Pickles
One Two Three

Deep Thoughts

Chapter 1

My phone rang.

"Hello," I said. "Flytrap Detective Agency."

A gruff voice started barking questions at me.

"You solve mysteries—right, bud?"

"I am not a bud. I am a fully grown Venus flytrap," I replied.

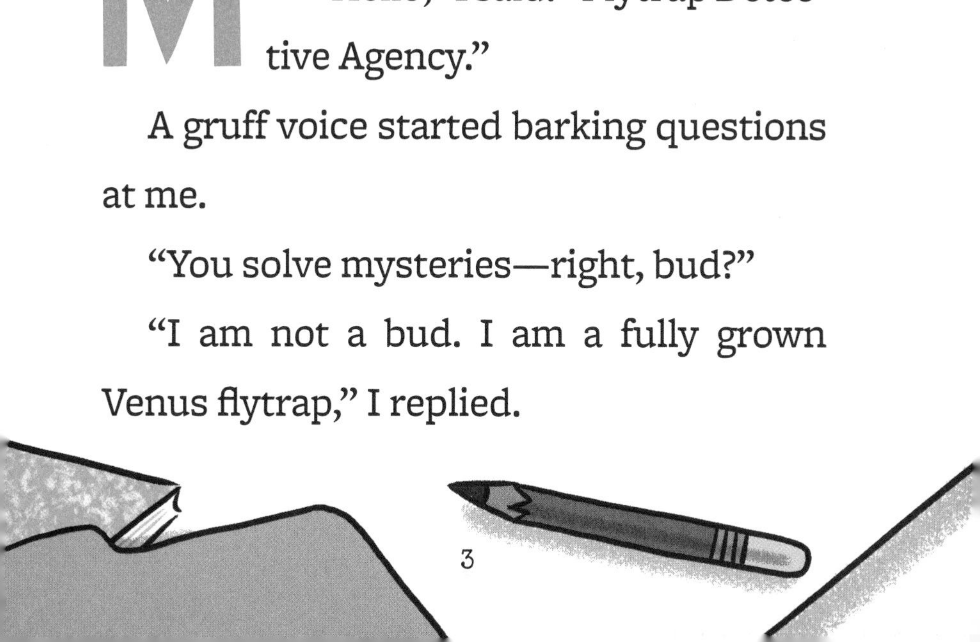

"A Venus flytrap? Isn't that one of those plants that can eat flies?"

"Yes," I replied. "I eat flies, and I also solve mysteries. But I only solve the world's greatest mysteries."

"Huh?" growled the voice.

"I want to be the World's Greatest Detective," I said. "So I've decided to solve only the world's greatest mysteries from now on. Is your mystery one of the world's greatest mysteries?"

"Uh, well," whimpered the voice. "We're putting on a dog show, and someone stole an invitation to compete in it."

"Hmm," I said. "That sounds more like a paperwork problem than one of the world's greatest mysteries. I'm sorry, but I can't help you."

"Please!" howled the voice.

"Oh, okay. I'll keep my eyes open for it."

"You have eyes? I thought you were a plant."

"Yes, I'm a plant, with eyes, a mouth, and leafy hands. Now—"

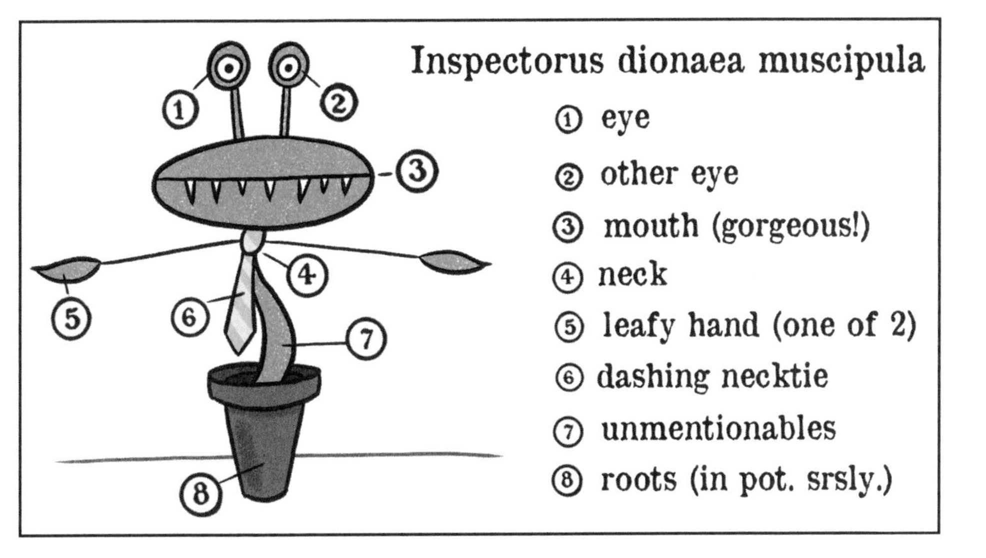

"What about feet? Do you have feet?"

"No, I have roots," I said.

"Then how do you go around investigating mysteries?"

"Well, it's none of your business, but I have a goat who pushes me on a skateboard," I said. "Now, if you'll excuse me, that goat is about to eat my new necktie. Goodbye."

"You have a neck?"

I hung up!

"Nina, please stop eating my tie!" I said. "It was very expensive!"

"Big deal," said Nina, but she stopped.

"Can you believe that person called me about a missing piece of paper?"

"Mmm, paper!" said Nina.

Nina the Goat is my assistant. She pushes me around so I can solve crimes. She is a goat. Goats are famous for eating almost anything. But for Nina there is no "almost." She eats EVERYTHING—

plastic buckets, metal cans, glass bottles, straw hats, wooden cabinets, cotton underwear, and whatever it is telephones are made out of! She really seems to like that.

"Nina! Stop eating the telephone! It could ring at any second with news of a brand-new world's greatest mystery for me to solve!"

"Big meal."

Chapter 2

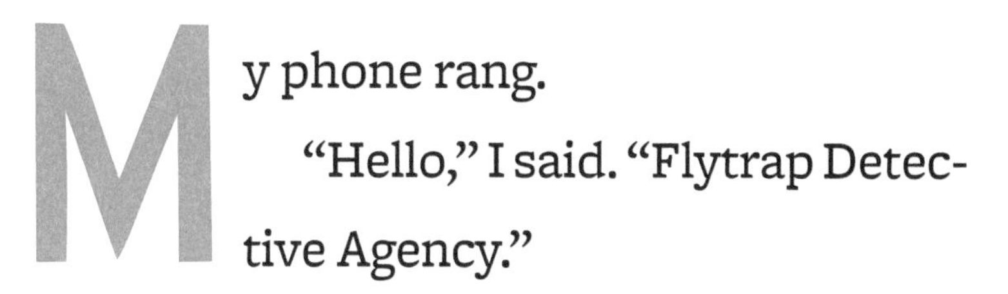

My phone rang.

"Hello," I said. "Flytrap Detective Agency."

A very fancy voice started bossing me around.

"Flytrap, you must come down to the train station right away! My pickle paperweight has been stolen!"

"Sorry," I said. "I have already found

missing pickle paperweights twice before. Now that I am solving only the world's greatest mysteries, I cannot waste any more time on pickle paperweights."

"But this is the world's GREATEST pickle paperweight," the fancy voice insisted. "It's a solid-gold pickle that's encrusted with emeralds, diamonds, and moon rocks, and I recently bought it for 100 million dollars!"

"I'll be right there," I said and hung up.

"Nina! The game is afoot! We have a world's greatest mystery to solve!"

"Big deal," said Nina, swallowing the rest of my tie.

Chapter 3

The World's Greatest Detective needs to look good. So I put on a new tie.

Then Nina helped me onto my skateboard and began pushing me to the train station.

Normally, it's pretty scary when she pushes me through the city, because she is not as careful of traffic as she should be. I have nearly been run over by cars, trucks, buses, and, once, a nun on roller skates.

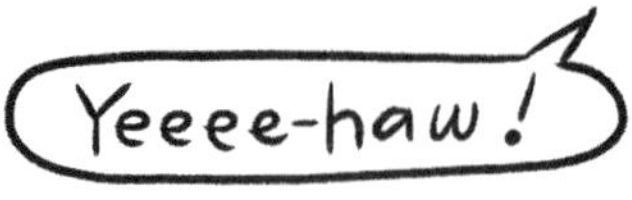

But this time everybody stopped to let us pass because they could hear us coming. SQUEAK SQUEAK SQUEAK

"Nina!" I shouted. "One of the skateboard wheels is squeaking!"

"Big squeal," agreed Nina.

"Well," I said, "I think it's more of a squeak. What should we do about it?"

"Eat it?" asked Nina.

"NO!" I shouted. "Then we'll never get to the train station to solve the mystery of the world's greatest pickle paperw—"

“We’re there,” interrupted Nina.

She stopped the skateboard so quickly that my pot went flying across the train station and landed sideways in front of a very fancy poodle.

“Greetings,” said the very fancy poodle. “I am the Countess Zuzu Poodle-doo. And you must be the . . . the World’s Greatest Detective?”

"I'm—*urgh!*—working on it," I said, struggling to get my pot upright. "And—*yurgh!*—now I am—*blurgh!*—working on your case."

"My butler will help you," said the Countess.

The butler, a very serious looking Chihuahua, picked me up, dusted off my pot, and placed it back on my skateboard.

"Thank you!" I said. "Also, I apologize for the fact that my goat is eating your top hat."

“Very good, sir,” said the butler, very properly putting the half-eaten hat back on his head.

“My name is Inspector Flytrap, and this is my assistant, Nina the Goat. She’s a goat.”

“Very good, sir,” said the butler, very politely. “My name is MC FunkyFoot, and I am at your service.”

“MC FunkyFoot seems like a strange name for a butler,” I said.

“My parents always dreamed that I’d be a rap star,” said MC FunkyFoot.

"Mister FunkyFoot! Would you *please* stop talking about things other than my pickle paperweight?" screeched the Countess. "Inspector Flytrap needs to get right to work!"

"Very good, ma'am," MC FunkyFoot and I said at the same time.

"I just arrived by train," said the Countess. "But my world's greatest pickle paperweight was stolen during the trip! Your job is to find it! So get busy!"

I could tell already that the Countess liked for things to go her way, and her way only. I hoped she wouldn't notice that Nina was eating the flowers off her hat.

The EPIC STORY of MC Funky Foot
MC Funky Foot! That's his NAME — And breaking beats — that's his GAME!
He'll scratch some GROOVES And bust some MOVES!
HUA
THE NEW AND BEST SYSTEM FOR DELIVERING MILK
10 years later, at the SCHOOL O'RAP...
MC Funky, your rhymes got NOTHING! But you're polite, and that's saying SOMETHING!
MY RAP
D+
Roses are red
Violets are blue
I like white gloves
And pouring tea
Very good, sir. I polished your silver.
Awww...
At graduation from the SCHOOL O'RAP...
I lack the skills to be a rapper. I would like to be a butler.
That's OK, MC FUNKY! Just because your rhymes are CLUNKY Does not mean you can't PURSUE your but-but-butler dreams so TRUE!
HUA
Very GOOD, sir!
*This floor is so shiny thanks to ANOTHER FINE WAXING JOB™ by MC Funky Foot!

Chapter 4

"And now," said the Countess, "my personal policewoman will tell you about the crime."

"Yo, I'm Sergeant Sniff," said a tough-looking Pekingese. "See, the Countess just bought the gold pickle in Fancitonia. Then we brought it back here on this choo-choo."

"You mean the train?"

"Yes."

"I wish you wouldn't call it a choo-choo," I said. "It is a fine example of a mountain-type 4-8-4 streamlined steam-powered Z-class standard gauge New York & Montreal Express locomotive, one of the most advanced machines ever built."

"Big wheel," said Nina, nibbling at a brake line.

"Flytrap!" yapped the Countess. "Would you PLEASE focus on my pickle paperweight?"

"Oh, yes, of course!" I said. "Where is it?"

"It's MISSING, you fool!"

"Er, sorry. I meant: Where WAS it?"

"This way," said Sergeant Sniff. "It was locked inside this armored boxcar before we left Fancitonia." She pointed to a box-

car with thick walls. It looked like a big bank safe on wheels. The door was open, and I noticed cameras and laser beams inside.

"When we pulled into the station, the gold pickle was gone!" continued Sergeant Sniff. "The thief struck while the choo-choo was choo-chooing down the choo-choo track!"

"What about the cameras and the laser-beam alarms? Didn't they catch the thief?"

"Obviously not," said Sergeant Sniff, glaring at me. "The cameras only picked up a blur, and the thief somehow dodged all the laser beams."

"Nina, please wheel me over so I can have a closer look," I said.

Nina pushed me over to the boxcar—way too fast, as usual—then jumped up on the back of the locomotive and started eating the coal.

"Hmm," I said, examining the floor of the boxcar. "Look at these scratches! Are these dog claw marks?"

"They are claw marks, but not from a dog," said Sergeant Sniff. "The police lab says they were made by something bigger and tougher than a dog claw."

"Hmm . . . Who else was on the train?"

"Just us," said Sergeant Sniff. "The Countess and I were the only passengers. And MC FunkyFoot was driving the train."

"So," I said, "if the thief wasn't on the train when it left the first station and wasn't on the train when it got to this station, then he must have gotten aboard the train while it was moving, stolen the pickle, and gotten back off again."

"Isn't that what I said a minute ago?" snarled Sergeant Sniff. "The choo-choo bandit got on the choo-choo while it as choo-chooing from the choo-choo station to—"

"AHA!" I interrupted. "I have solved the World's Greatest Mystery!"

Chapter 5

"Who did it?" shouted the Countess Zuzu Poodle-doo.

"Who did it?" murmured the butler, MC FunkyFoot, very properly.

"Who did it?" demanded Sergant Sniff.

"Yum yum, this coal is dee-licious!" said Nina.

"Nina, stop eating the coal. It's a precious natural resource!" I shouted.

"Would you stop shouting at that goat and tell us who did it?" said everybody.

"Well," I admitted, "I can't tell you exactly WHO did it, but I can give you a description."

"I guess that's better than nothing," said Sergeant Sniff, taking out a notebook. "Go ahead."

"First," I said. "The criminal must be very fast to be just a blur on the camera."

"Hmm," said Sergeant Sniff, looking around the train station.

"Second, the criminal must be very nimble to dodge all those laser-beam alarms."

"Hmmmm!" said Sergeant Sniff, gazing in the general direction of Nina.

"Third, the criminal must be very sure-footed to jump on and off a moving train."

"Hmmmmmm!" said Sergeant Sniff, staring right at Nina.

"And, finally," I said, "the thief is not a dog but is an animal with large, tough claws or even . . . hooves."

"HMMMM!" said Sergeant Sniff, glaring into Nina's big brown eyes.

"OH NO!" I shouted.

"What's the problem?" asked Nina. And she very smoothly jumped off the locomotive, nimbly took another bite out of the butler's hat while in mid-air, and sure-footedly landed on her hooves.

"YOU are under arrest for the theft of the golden pickle paperweight!" hollered Sergeant Sniff, snapping a pair of hoof-cuffs around Nina's front legs.

"Big steal," said Nina.

FREE
NINA!

PART 2
Inspector Flytrap in The Slow and the Furious

SS FUZZ

Chapter 6

It was a big steal—I mean, deal!

A whole squad of police officers showed up with police cars, a police helicopter, and a police boat. (Since there was no water nearby, they had to tow the boat behind one of the cars.)

Worst of all was the police goat wagon!

They loaded Nina in it and took her away . . . to jail!

"Nina! I'll solve the crime! Don't eat their police hats—they don't like that. I'll get you out of jail!" I called.

In a moment it was all over. Sergeant Sniff and the police were gone. The Countess and her butler were gone. And, of course, Nina was gone.

Everybody was gone! Except for a sloth reading a newspaper.

"Gee . . . ," said the sloth, slowly. "I'd call this . . . one of the World's Greatest . . . Mysteries!"

"You're right!" I cried. "And I, Inspector Flytrap, swear that I will not stop until I have solved it!"

"Okay," said the sloth, slowly. "See you . . . later."

"OH NO!" I cried. "I just realized that I can't solve the mystery."

"The criminal is . . . too smart for you?" the sloth asked.

"Of course not!" I yelled. "But without Nina, I can't GO anywhere!"

"I . . . could . . . push you," said the sloth, slowly.

"Really?" I asked. "That is so kind of you!"

"Sure," said the sloth, slowly. "Where do you want to go?"

I realized that I didn't know where to go! I needed to track down the actual gold pickle thief. And the real gold pickle thief was obviously a Master Criminal!

But Master Criminals are really good at hiding, which is what makes them Master Criminals.

I had gotten the world's greatest mystery I had always wanted, but now I had no idea who did it, how to find them, or even where to start looking!

Chapter 7

My cell phone rang.

"Hello," I said. "Inspector Flytrap speaking."

"This is Koko Dodo," said a crazy voice. "I need your help!"

"I thought you were mad at me," I said.

"No! Never again! Well . . . not if you can help me," said Koko Dodo, sounding desperate. "Last night a Master Criminal stole all of my gourmet cookie sprinkles!"

"The chocolate ones or the rainbow ones?" I asked.

"ALL OF THEM!"

"I'll be right there!" I said.

AHA! Now I was on the trail of the Master Criminal!

"Come, Mr. Sloth, the game is afoot! Please take me to Koko Dodo's Cookie Shop. As fast as possible! It's a gourmet emergency!"

The sloth started to push me. Really, really slowly.

I know I have always complained about Nina pushing me too fast, but too slow is actually worse!

After thirty-five minutes, we had gone only a half a block from the train station.

We passed a TV store that had a big TV on display in the window. On the TV was a turkey news reporter standing outside of the city jail.

“This is Greta Von Hopinstop, reporting for CNNNNNNM News. I’m here at the city jail trying to get a comment from Nina the Goat, who has just been arrested for the Theft of the Century!”

Greta held her microphone up to a barred window.

“Nina the Goat! You could be sent to jail for the rest of your life for stealing the golden pickle paperweight! Do you have a comment?”

Nina stuck her tongue out from between the bars.

“Big deal,” she said.

A message flashed across the bottom of the screen: TONIGHT AT 11:00—WHEN GOATS GO BAAAAD!

Chapter 8

While I was still on my way to Koko Dodo's, my phone rang again.

"Hello," I said. "Inspector Flytrap speaking."

"This is Lulu Emu," said a beautiful voice.

"I thought you were mad at me," I said.

"No! Never again! Well . . . not if you

can help me," said Lulu Emu. "Last night a Master Criminal stole our most priceless painting!"

"*The Mona Spaghetti*?"

"No, that's not priceless anymore—ever since your goat ate the spaghetti part."

"Oh, yeah," I said.

"The stolen painting is a masterpiece by Michelangelo called *The Sistine Chapstick*!"

"I'll be right there!" I said.

AHA! Now I was on the trail of the Master Criminal! But now the trail was longer, and my sloth seemed to be getting slower!

"Let's go, Mr. Sloth! Please take me to art museum instead. As quickly as possible! It's an art emergency!"

The sloth turned me around and started to push me in the other direction. Really, really slowly.

We passed by the TV store again.

On the TV, Greta Von Hopinstop was still standing in front of the jail with her microphone.

"Nina the Goat, the Supreme Court has just ruled that you must stay in jail forever and ever and ever. Do you have a comment?"

"Big deal," said Nina.

A message flashed across the bottom of the screen: BREAKING NEWS: GOAT SAYS SAME THING AGAIN!

Chapter 9

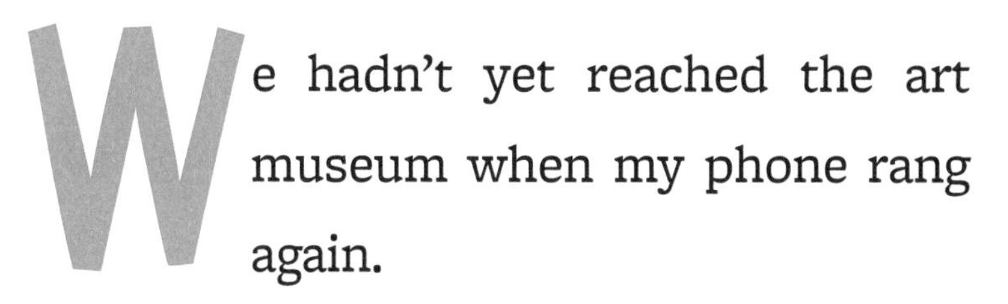

We hadn't yet reached the art museum when my phone rang again.

"Hello," I said. "Inspector Flytrap speaking."

"Tryflap? This is President Horse G. Horse," said a rude voice.

"I thought you were mad at me," I said.

"Of course I'm mad at you!" said President Horse. "But I still need your help, Flyblap. Last night a Master Criminal stole our most valuable presidential limousine, the Ford Ford!"

"I'll be right there!" I said.

AHA! Now I was . . . well, still on the really long trail of the Master Criminal! And now it was even longer!

"Mr. Sloth! Please take me to the White House instead. It's a national emergency!"

Slowly, even more slowly than before, he turned me around and started pushing me in the other direction.

We passed the TV store again. Now Nina was eating Greta Von Hopinstop's microphone and Greta was trying to reach through the barred window and hit Nina with her shoe. A message flashed across the bottom of the screen: PLEASE STAND BY. WE ARE EXPERIENCING TECHNICAL DIFFICULTIES.

Chapter 10

On the way to the White House, my phone rang.

It was twenty-three scientific pigs. A Master Criminal had stolen their Computatotron 80001 supercomputer!

My phone rang again.

It was a pegleg pirate who was missing his treasure map!

My phone rang again.

It was Mimi Kiwi. A Master Criminal had stolen every plant from her garden!

My phone rang again.

It was Vanessa Cowcow. A Master Criminal had stolen her sculpture . . . while she was working on it!

My phone rang again.

It was the dog from the dog show checking about the missing entry form.

"I'm sorry! I can't do everything!" I yelled into the phone and hung up.

"Actually . . . I can't do ANYTHING," I said. "This Master Criminal is so far ahead of me, I'll never catch up. He or she is the World's Greatest Thief and is creating the world's greatest mysteries . . . but I . . . I am not the World's Greatest Detective. I will never say 'AHA' again."

I was interrupted by the sloth, wheezing and gasping for breath. "Wheeze! Gasp! This high-speed chase is wearing me out! I'm so tired and hungry I can't go on."

Meanwhile, on the TeeVee...
Coming up: Nina the Goat sings the BIG DEAL PRISON BLUES! But first, a word from our SPONSOR!
Are you feeling DOWN? Are you kinda BLAH? Are you...
...the WORLD'S WORST DETECTIVE?
TRY THIS!
THE CELEBRATED
CREAM O' WHATSIT®
YUM YUM YUM
CREAM O' WHATSIT® will make you feel like your old self again™! But don't take MY word for it-
I drank 73 GALLONS of CREAM O' WHATSIT®...
...and now I feel like my old self again™!
CREAM O' WHATSIT®- Exactly what you NEED™!

GRUMBLE WUMBLE WOOOOO

PART 3

Inspector Flytrap Does NOT Have Lunch

OPEN

Chapter 11

I looked around.

The sloth had stopped right in front of Penguini's Linguini, my favorite restaurant!

And there was Penguini!

"Penguini! Can you fix up some sloth food to help out Mr. Sloth here?"

"No!"

No? What was happening? Penguini is always happy to see me and always happy to serve customers.

“Last night a Master Criminal stole all of my pots and pans!”

“Maybe just a snack from the refrigerator, then?” I said.

“The Master Criminal stole the refrigerator!”

“Can we dig through the trash?”

"The Master Criminal stole that, too! All he left me was one broken automatic pasta maker. Oh, Inspector Flytrap! It's too much! I'm closing my restaurant . . . FOREVER!"

Penguini locked the door of his restaurant and waddled off.

WOOF.
MOST PICKLE-LIKE
DAWG
CREAM O' WHATSIT
SOUR
MILK

PART 4

Inspector Flytrap in The Good, the Bad, and the Trash Heap

RESIDENTIAL

Chapter 12

My phone rang.

"Flytrap! Darling!" said the loveliest voice ever.

"Wanda!" I cried.

It was my girlfriend, Wanda. Wanda is a rose.

That's when I had a great idea! An idea that could help me catch the Master

Criminal! Maybe I COULD become the World's Greatest Detective after all!

See, Wanda is also a plant in a pot.

She also needs help getting around.

William the Goat pushes Wanda around on a skateboard. So if William—who is Nina's boyfriend— would push ME around instead, I could get back on the trail of the Master Criminal, find all of the missing stuff, and free Nina!

"Wanda, could I—" I began.

"Oh, Flytrap!" she interrupted. "It's so awful! A Master Criminal has kidnapped William the Goat!"

Chapter 13

That was it.

My last hope.

Now it was all over.

I'd never, ever, ever find the Master Criminal.

"By the way," said the sloth, not all that slowly. "I am the Master Criminal."

Chapter 14

"WHAT?" I said.

"Yep, it's me," the sloth said. And again he wasn't talking slowly at all. If anything he was talking SLIGHTLY FAST!

"But . . . but . . . but the Master Criminal is fast! And nimble! And sure-footed! The Master Criminal has big claws or hooves. The Master Criminal is totally evil!"

"All true," he said.

Very quickly, the sloth leapt onto the wall of Penguini's restaurant! Using his big slothy claws, he scampered up the building, disappeared into a window.

Seconds later, the door of Penguini's restaurant was kicked open and the sloth walked out, carrying a broken automatic pasta maker.

"I almost missed this one!" he said. "Sometimes it's tough to be TOTALLY evil. You really have to be careful or you wind up missing something. Then you've only been partly evil. And that's just not good enough for a Master Criminal like myself."

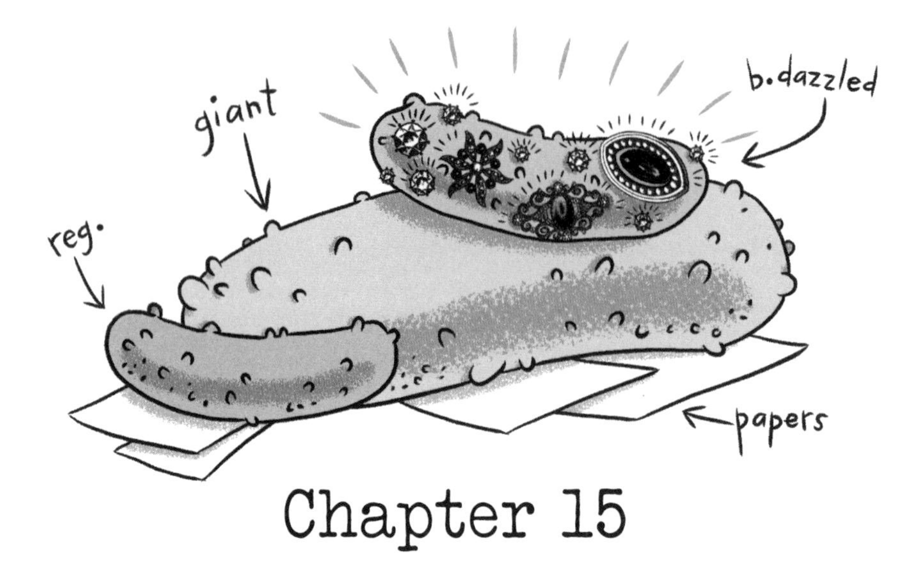

Chapter 15

"But why? Why do these evil deeds at all?" I demanded.

"I never wanted to be a Master Criminal . . . not at first. But YOU drove me to it, Flytrap!"

"*Me?* What did I do?"

"At first, all I wanted was to steal a regular pickle paperweight. But you and your goat got in my way!"

"That was you?"

"Yes! Then I tried to steal the GIANT pickle paperweight! You and your goat got in my way again!"

"That was you?"

"YES! So this time, when I saw my chance to steal the golden pickle paper-weight, I decided to get rid of you AND your goat!"

"Well," I sneered, "you got my goat out of the way, but now, I, Inspector Flytrap, the World's Greatest Detective, have caught you!"

"Oh, Flytrap," giggled the sloth, "I'm afraid it's the other way around. I, Sloth, the World's Greatest Master Criminal, have caught YOU!"

As fast as a lightning bolt, he grabbed my phone and flung it on the sidewalk. *Klonk!* It burst into fifty-seven pieces!

As fast as a striking snake, he swung

one of his big slothy claws at my flower-pot. *Crack!* The pot split in half, and all the dirt—and all of me—spilled out onto the ground!

As fast as the fastest sloth that ever lived, he grabbed my skateboard, jumped on, and rode away.

"Har har de har har de har har!" he laughed with an evil slothy laugh.

Chapter 16

My phone didn't ring! It couldn't!

The Master Criminal was free to continue his crime spree, and I had no way of even knowing what was happening.

Now I had really lost everything!

I had no phone!

No skateboard!

No flowerpot!

NO NINA!

"I need Nina!" I wailed.

"That IS a big deal," Nina said.

"Nina! Is it really you?"

"Yepth," she said with her mouth full. She was busy eating the remains of my phone.

Yes, it really WAS her!

"I thought you were in jail!"

"Ate it."

"You mean you ate through the bars of your jail cell and escaped?"

"Big steel," Nina said, and belched.

"Oh, Nina!" I cried and tried to throw my leafy arms around her neck.

"Sloth's getting away," she announced.

"OH MY FLIES!" I cried. "You're right! Let's go!"

But then I remembered my stolen skateboard. "It's no use," I said. "The sloth has my skateboard. We can't catch him."

Nina picked me up with one of her dainty hooves, shook the dirt out of my roots, and tossed me up onto her back.

"No cowboy jokes," said Nina.

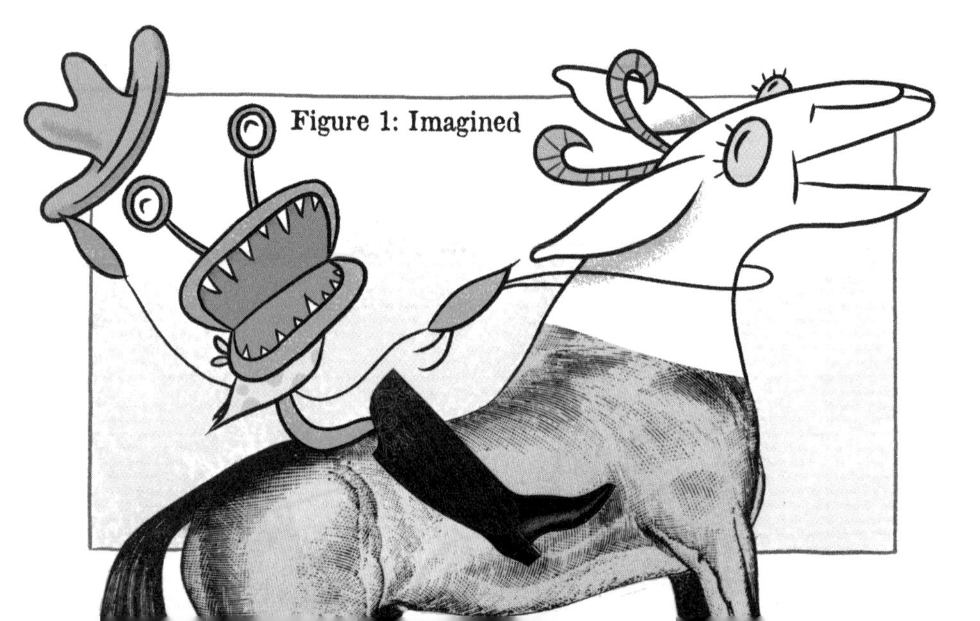

But I couldn't help it. I was just too excited about being back in action again!

"Hi-ho, Nina! AWAY!" I yelled.

Nina did not rear up on her hind legs like the Lone Ranger's horse. Nina did not whinny with the fury of the chase like the Lone Ranger's horse. Nina did not run like the wind with thundering hooves like the Lone Ranger's horse.

"Where to?" she asked, chewing on some of the flowerpot dirt.

That's when I realized I didn't know where to go. The sloth was way out of sight by now.

But then I had an idea!

"The sloth has my skateboard! So we CAN catch him! Nina, use your super strong goat hearing. Do you hear it?"

Nina's ears twitched.

"Tiny squeal."

"Yes! That's it! The squeaking wheel of my skateboard!" I said. "Nina, follow that squeal!"

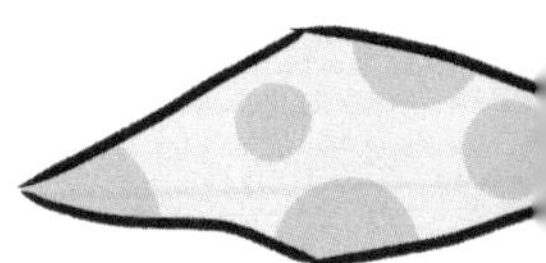

Nina trotted off at a brisk pace.

"Oh," I said. "I forgot to tell you. The sloth kidnapped your boyfriend, William."

Nina reared up on her hind legs!

Nina whinnied with the fury of the chase!

Nina ran like the wind with thundering hooves!

"Yeeeee-haw!" I yelled, hanging on for dear life.

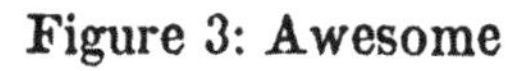

Figure 3: Awesome

Chapter 17

Sheesh! Riding like the wind and listening to thundering hooves can really give you a headache!

Even worse, just when we thought we were about to catch the sloth, the squeaking stopped!

Nina skidded to a halt and listened carefully.

"Nope," she said. "He stopped."

EVERYTHANG'S A SLOTH DOLLAR!

"He must be nearby!" I said. "Maybe he went into one of these buildings!"

I looked around.

There was a theater showing *Sloth Luv Story*.

A cafeteria was featuring "All the sloth food you can eat!"

A beauty parlor was advertising "Let us paint your sloth toe claws in rainbow glitter!"

A store was selling "Pinstripe suits for the well-dressed sloth!"

A newsboy was yelling, "*Sloth News*! Get your *Sloth News*!"

And a dog show.

"AHA!" I shouted and it felt really good to yell "AHA" again. "I know where he is! He's hiding in the—"

"Dog show?" asked Nina.

"Yes," I said. "How did you know?"

"Stolen entry form," said Nina.

"Well done, Nina!" I said. "Let's go!"

Nina galloped into the dog show.

"Wow, that's one ugly dog," said the dog selling tickets. He pointed at Nina.

Nina ate the tickets and kept going.

We burst into the main arena. There were hundreds of dogs! Every one with beautiful makeup and lovely fluffy fur! And every one different!

One of them must be the sloth. But which one? There was so much lovely fluffy fur I couldn't tell!

There must be some way to separate a sloth from all these dogs . . .

LOOKiT ALL THE DAWGS at the DAWG SHOW!
BUFFY
BOFFY
BiFFY
YAW HAW
OOBY OO
PUDDLES
HER HIGHNESS POLLY WOLLY DOODLE OF BACON AND EGGS ON TOAST (WITH JELLY, ALSO) IV
DUSTY
MUSTY
CRUSTY
GARY
THIS CAN'T BE GOOD...
TUFF STUFF
BURP.
BURPALOTTA

“AHA!” I yelled. “I’ve got it.”

I grabbed the judge’s microphone.

“SIT!”

Every dog and one sloth sat. The audience applauded, and the judges scribbled on their clipboards.

“SPEAK!”

Every dog and one sloth barked. The audience applauded, and the judges scribbled on their clipboards.

“ROLL OVER!”

Every dog and one sloth rolled over. The audience applauded, and the judges scribbled on their clipboards.

“HANG UPSIDE DOWN!”

Every dog just sat there, but the sloth nimbly jumped onto the big DOG SHOW banner and hung upside down. The audience applauded, and the judges scribbled on their clipboards.

"THERE HE IS! LET'S GET HIM!" I yelled.

I meant to just say this to Nina. But I forgot that I was holding the microphone!

Instantly, every dog and Nina leapt forward and began chasing the sloth! The judges were chasing him, too . . . with a trophy!

Chapter 18

The sloth swung into the air, did a perfect back flip, landed on MY skateboard, and zoomed out the exit!

Nina, the pack of show dogs, the judges, the audience members, and I raced out to the street after him.

The sloth dodged cars, trucks, trolleys, and a very large statue of President Horse G. Horse, and so did we.

Then we saw President Horse himself.

"There goes the thief who stole your limo!" I shouted.

So the president started galloping along with us.

Nina and I were almost run down by a pickup truck going the other way. I turned to yell at the driver and saw it was

Mimi Kiwi . . . who was already yelling at us!

"There goes the thief who stole your garden!" I shouted.

Mimi Kiwi screeched into a tight U-turn, gunned the engine, and joined the chase.

We passed the art museum, where Vanessa Cowcow and Lulu Emu were

about to unveil a statue called *The Ice Cream Truck Made out of Cheese*.

"There goes the thief who stole *The Sistine Chapstick*!" I shouted.

They both hopped into *The Ice Cream Truck Made out of Cheese* and joined the chase.

Then we passed Koko Dodo's Cookie Shop, where twenty-three scientific pigs were mad that Koko Dodo had run out of gourmet cookie sprinkles.

"There goes the thief who stole the gourmet cookie sprinkles!" I shouted.

“The chocolate ones or the rainbow ones?” shouted back twenty-three pigs and one dodo.

“ALL OF THEM!”

The pigs hopped onto twenty-three tricycles, and Koko Dodo put on her jetpack, and they all joined the chase.

As we zoomed through downtown, I saw Penguini hanging a CLOSED FOREVER sign on his food truck!

"There goes the thief who stole your pots, pans, refrigerator, and broken automatic pasta maker!" I shouted.

Penguini leapt into the food truck, gunned the engine, and joined the chase!

We passed a construction site. I saw my girlfriend, Wanda, busy at her new job, driving a high-speed bulldozer.

"Wanda! Darling! There goes the thief who kidnapped William!"

BARRROOOOM! She fired up the big bulldozer and joined the chase!

We went over a bridge, and I saw a giant pegleg pirate in a giant pirate ship.

“There goes the thief who stole your giant pickle paperweight!” I shouted.

“Meh,” said the pirate, and he went back to painting pretty unicorns on his pegleg.

We just barely missed a head-on collision with the Countess Poodle-doo’s old-timey limousine.

“There goes the thief who stole the golden pickle paperweight!” I shouted.

MC FreakyFoot, the Countess’s butler and chauffeur, put the limo in reverse. Then he, the Countess, and Sergeant Sniff joined the chase, backwards at full speed!

Very good, sir.
ICE CREAM
PASTA!
PENGUINI'S
CREAM O' WHATSIT
This can't be good...

Now we were an unstoppable tidal wave of justice! Dogs, barnyard animals, flightless birds, two plants, and a variety of potentially dangerous vehicles!

And we were gaining on the Master Criminal!

Chapter 19

"What's that sign say?" I asked.

"Whblch oneblh?" Nina asked.

"The one you're eating!"

"Big Yield," said Nina.

"Ah, a large Yield sign," I said. "I notice that the word *Yield* is followed by three exclamation points and the words *Danger! Danger! Danger!* I wonder what we're supposed to yield to."

Nina coughed up part of the sign.

There was more to it.

"Let's see here . . ." I said. "Ah, yes, it says, 'YIELD to garbage trucks! City dump ahead! Garbage trucks only! Go slow! Be extremely careful because you're almost to the place where trucks dump the garbage over the side of the huge cliff into the big garbage pit! Slam on your brakes! OH NO! LOOKOUT! Forget about yielding, just STOP!!!!!'"

But it was way too late to stop now!

We had caught up with the sloth right at the edge of the World's Biggest Garbage Pit!

Chapter 20

"I've got him!" I shouted, reaching out with my longest leaf and grabbing the sloth.

"NO, YOU DON'T!" yelled the sloth.

And he swerved the skateboard, hit a ramp, and went high into the air . . . and over the edge of the cliff.

But I held on tight—actually, I couldn't unwind my leaf in time—and was dragged after him!

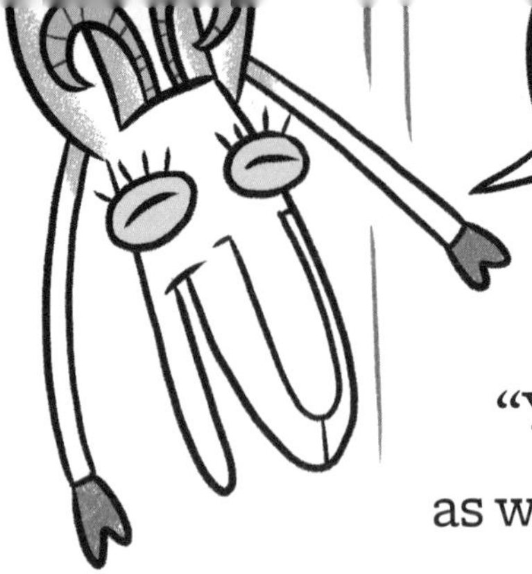

"YEEEE-HAW!" I shouted as we plunged over the edge of the cliff toward the big, giant, huge, enormous, stinky city dump!

"YEEEE-HAW!" shouted Nina as she leapt after us with her fast, sure-footed, and nimble hooves! "YEEEE-HAW!" shouted President Horse, Vanessa Cowcow, Lulu Emu, Penguini, Koko Dodo, twenty-three pig scientists, the Countess, the butler, the police dog, my beautiful girlfriend, Wanda, and all the show dogs as they zoomed, swooshed, rumbled, and pedaled after us! (Actually, the pigs all said "Oinnnnnnk!")

Chapter 21

Kersmash!!

Chapter 22

It took a long time to sort everything out after that.

Or perhaps I should say, DIG everything out.

Luckily, Wanda's bulldozer had landed safely on an old sofa, so she was able to clear away a lot of the wrecked cars, trucks, tricycles, etc.

And at the bottom of it all . . . I still had a tight grip on the sloth!

We had landed in a Dumpster filled with stolen priceless artwork, gourmet cookie sprinkles, linguini pans, a used presidential limo, a lovely garden, William the Goat, and a solid-gold jewel-encrusted pickle paperweight!!!!!

"AHA!" I shouted. "I've caught the Master Criminal AND found the secret hideout where he hid all of your stuff!"

Everyone cheered! Wanda gave me a big kiss! The pigs lifted me in the air!

And just as the TV news crews arrived, the President made an announcement.

"Attention, everyone here at the city dump or watching this on television!" he proclaimed. "This fine plant, Inspector Flytrap, is officially the World's Greatest Detective!"

"NO!" someone shouted.

The cheering stopped. Everyone looked around to see who had yelled no.

It was me.

"WE," I said, putting a leaf around Nina, "are the World's Greatest Detective . . . Team!"

"Big feels," said Nina, and she wiped away a tear with her hoof.

Chapter 23

My phone rang.

"Hello," I said. "Flytrap and Goat Detective Agency. This is Inspector Flytrap speaking."

An excited voice told me about the greatest, most thrilling, BIG DEAL mystery ever!

"I'm sorry," I said. "Nina and I are currently on vacation here at the city dump.

We look forward to solving your mystery in two or three weeks . . . after Nina finishes eating."

I hung up the phone and leaned back in my new pot—a priceless Grecian urn given to me by the art museum—and enjoyed the peace and quiet.

Well, quiet except for the buzzing of the countless flies that swarmed around the dump.

Mmmmm . . . Tasty, tasty flies!

ABOUT THE AUTHOR

TOM ANGLEBERGER is the author of the best-selling Origami Yoda series, as well as *Fake Mustache* and *Horton Halfpott*, both Edgar Award nominees, the Qwikpick Papers series, and *Fuzzy*, with Paul Dellinger. Visit Tom online at origamiyoda.com.

ABOUT THE ILLUSTRATOR

CECE BELL is the author of the *New York Times* bestselling *El Deafo*, which won a Newbery Honor. She is also the author of The Rabbit and Robot books. Tom and Cece are married and live in Christiansburg, Virginia.